Phantasmal Chronicles

A Collection of Eerie Tales

Sayan Panda

Ukiyoto Publishing

All global publishing rights are held by

Ukiyoto Publishing

Published in 2024

Content Copyright © Sayan Panda

ISBN 9789362694645

All rights reserved.

No part of this publication may be reproduced, transmitted, or stored in a retrieval system, in any form by any means, electronic, mechanical, photocopying, recording or otherwise, without the prior permission of the publisher.

The moral rights of the author have been asserted.

This is a work of fiction. Names, characters, businesses, places, events, locales, and incidents are either the products of the author's imagination or used in a fictitious manner. Any resemblance to actual persons, living or dead, or actual events is purely coincidental.

This book is sold subject to the condition that it shall not by way of trade or otherwise, be lent, resold, hired out or otherwise circulated, without the publisher's prior consent, in any form of binding or cover other than that in which it is published.

www.ukiyoto.com

To Jhummi

Contents

The Old Graveyard	1
Companion	5
The Dead of Night	8
Overtime	13
Pyres Burning	19
The Knock at the Door	24
The Divine Manuscript	29
The Curious Case of Malati Sen	37
Missing	44
The Old School	49
About the Author	*54*

The Old Graveyard

Shuken sighed as he gazed across the vast expanse of tombstones that lay before him. It was his first night serving as the watchman for the old graveyard situated behind St. Mary's Church, a centuries-old place of worship located on the edge of town.

As the sun dipped below the horizon, painting the sky in hues of orange and pink, Shuken felt a sense of loneliness settle over him. He had always been a skeptic when it came to tales of ghosts and supernatural occurrences. But spending an entire night alone in this quiet graveyard, surrounded by the dead, was enough to give anyone pause.

Shuken began his routine patrol, flashlight in hand, determined to carry out his duties in a efficient and logical manner. His breath created wisps of steam in the frigid evening air. As he walked, his light danced over weathered headstones listing at odd angles, many choked with weeds and overgrown moss. Carved names and dates were barely legible on some of the oldest markers.

The graveyard held a long history stretching back centuries. This small town had grown and changed around it, yet this final resting place had remained, enduring all manner of weather and the passage of time. Shuken tried to imagine all the lives represented in this soil, all the dramas and tribulations now long past. Who were these people in life? What stories did each grave hold?

A branch snapped in the nearby trees, pulled by the breeze, and Shuken jumped at the sudden noise piercing the stillness. He chided himself for being so jumpy, there was nothing to fear in this place. As he walked, his boots crunched over dead leaves and dry grass. The air was filled with an earthy, decaying scent.

Some distance away, at the edge of the woods bordering the graveyard, Shuken spotted two glowing eyes peering out from the darkness. He stiffened, senses on high alert, but after a long moment whatever animal it was silently slipped back into the forest. Shuken let out the breath he didn't realize he was holding. He was truly starting to let his imagination run wild out here.

Half of his shift passed without incident as Shuken continually swept his light over the gravestones. A sliver of moon had risen, casting the barest amount of pale light over the somber scene. Shuken was beginning to relax into a sort of trance when faint noises broke the stillness.

At first he dismissed it as another nocturnal animal stirring in the woods. But then the sound came again, and Shuken realized with a chill it was coming from somewhere within the graveyard itself. It was a scraping, clawing type of noise that raised the hairs on the back of his neck. Frozen in place, he scanned the flashlight beam over the nearest gravesites but saw nothing amiss.

The scratching came again, coming from somewhere off in the darkness. Shuken forced his feet to move, creeping cautiously in the direction of the horrible noise. As he drew nearer, it seemed to be emanating from a particularly old section of the graveyard where the markers were little more than weathered stumps jutting out of the earth.

Shuken paused a few feet away, afraid of what he might see but unable to stop himself from looking closer. His light roamed over the sunken grave plots until it fell upon a particular spot where the dirt was being raked back by some earthen talons jutting out from below the soil's surface.

Shuken let out an involuntary yell and leapt backwards, heart pounding, as a skeletal hand burst free of the grave, clawing at the empty air as if trying to pull the rest of the body up from below. For a long moment Shuken could only gape in horror, the beam of his flashlight dancing erratically across the gruesome sight.

Then, to his disbelief, the bony fingers sank back down into the loose dirt which shifted for a few moments as whatever was beneath continued its struggle to free itself from its centuries-old prison. Shuken scrambled backwards on hands and feet, wanting to put as much distance as possible between himself and that unholy grave.

Was this really happening? Had the stress and isolation of the job caused him to hallucinate something from his worst nightmares? Shuken sat with his back against a tree at the edge of the graveyard, flashlight clutched tightly, too afraid to re-approach that patch of disturbed earth but unable to leave his post.

He must have dozed from exhaustion because the next thing Shuken knew, faint gray light was filtering through the trees signaling the impending dawn. Stiff and disoriented, he climbed shakily to his feet. As he scanned the graveyard, he half-expected to see a figure lurching towards him but all lay still and silent once more.

Had he imagined the whole thing? Shuken couldn't be sure if he was losing his mind or if the old tales had some truth to them after all. He decided then and there this would be his first and last shift as night watchman. As the sunrise painted the sky rosy shades, he quit the job without a second glance back. For the first time, Shuken wondered if there really were forces beyond our normal understanding and if the departed ever truly found peace. His comfortable world of logic and reason had been shaken to the core last night, and the memory of that sightless gaze from within the grave would haunt him for years to come.

Companion

Shekhar was devastated. His loyal companion Toto had gone missing three days ago in the woods near their home. No amount of calling or searching turned up any clues to the little terrier's whereabouts. Late last night, a jogger had discovered Toto's body at the edge of the woods, barely recognizable under marks of violence.

The police had taken the body away after little more than a cursory inspection. "Dogs go missing all the time, it was probably another animal," the officer said dismissively before leaving. But Shekhar couldn't accept that. Toto had never wandered far from his side before. Something didn't feel right about his death.

Determined to get answers, Shekhar enlisted the help of his friends Raj, Dhruv and Aaryan. The four boys grew up exploring the woods together and knew every trail and hiding place within its leafy borders. After school that day, they gathered makeshift detective kits and headed to the scene of the discovery.

Under the shade of the trees, they searched inch by inch around the area, hoping to find any clues the police may have overlooked. "Look, drag marks in the dirt," Dhruv noticed. They led deeper into the woods, away from any usual animal trails. The boys followed doggedly (pun intended).

After a half hour of tracking, they came upon a small clearing. And their blood ran cold at what they saw. Piled in the centre were the remains of at least a dozen other dogs and cats in varying states of decay. Vicious slashes and broken bones told of unspeakable cruelty. "A serial killer," Aaryan whispered in panic.

They began to search the area more frantically now, hoping to find clues before the killer returned to dispose of more evidence. That's when Raj spotted something glinting under a bush. He pulled out an ornate knife with elaborate carvings on the handle. And embedded in the blade, traces of blood and fur. They had their first solid clue, but to a far more sinister crime than they imagined.

That evening, after consulting old newspapers at the library, they discovered a string of such killings two years ago that were never solved. The cryptic carvings on the handle led them to identify the culprit. Bilash Bihari Dutta, also known as Dutta Babu, had disappeared after neighbors reported screams from his rundown home.

The pieces were coming together, but the killer was still out there. And now the boys had put themselves on his trail. They knew they couldn't involve the authorities until they found more proof. Dutta Babu had eluded the police before. This time, it would take child detectives to bring a murderer to justice and gain closure for Toto.

Their search led them to the abandoned home on the outskirts of town. As they crept inside, the scent of death nearly overwhelmed them. A figure suddenly appeared at the top of the stairwell, hunched and wild-eyed. It was Dutta Babu, even more unhinged than his old wanted photos.

A desperate chase ensued through the tangled Property, but the boys knew the layout from old stories. They led the killer toward the deepest part of the woods, where an old system of animal traps still laid buried. With quick thinking, Dhruv was able to trigger one just as Dutta Babu lunged at them again.

The man's twisted screams echoed through the forest as the metal teeth clamped around his leg. Police sirens approached in the distance, drawn by the commotion. Justice for Toto and his other victims had finally been served by four young heroes. While a dark mystery had been unfolding all this while in their idyllic town, the future seemed a little brighter with such courageous souls to protect it.

The Dead of Night

Shubir dragged himself through the front doors of the Oakdale County Morgue, already exhausted at the prospect of a long night ahead. As the new night caretaker, it was his job to monitor the cold storage rooms, handle any unexpected deliveries from the local hospitals and emergency services, and generally ensure the peaceful slumber of the deceased residents was undisturbed.

"You'll be on your own after 8pm." Nurse Peters, the day shift supervisor, rattled off the closing procedures as she packed up to leave. "Any issues, call the contact number on the desk. Otherwise, hope you have a quiet one!" She winked, too cheerful for Shubir's liking, and waved goodbye.

Then he was alone. He double checked each of the heavy steel doors leading to the four storage rooms were secured, as per procedure. A flick through the records confirmed only a handful of long term residents remained on site. The majority had been claimed by grieving loved ones or released to the city crematorium to make space for fresh casualties.

With nothing left to do but wait, Shubir retreated to the small break room and attempted to lose himself in a book. But he couldn't settle, every creak of the old building setting his nerves on edge. At every small sound, he found himself eyeing the security camera screens warily, hoping to see nothing amiss in the shadowy corridors.

His anxiety spiked as midnight approached with no sign of the quiet night he'd been promised. A flurry of activity suddenly erupted outside - raised voices, hurried footsteps. Shubir jumped at the sound of fists pounding on the locked front doors. He let out a shaky breath when Nurse Peters' cheery face appeared, backlit by the glow of ambulance lights.

"Didn't think we'd leave you alone all night, did you?" She grinned, ushering in two porters who were wheeling a new arrival on a gurney. Shubir stammered a greeting and led them to Room 1, sliding back the heavy door.

"John Doe, late 50s. Died at the scene of an MVA." Nurse Peters rattled off the brief details as the porters transferred the shrouded body onto one of the empty shelves. "Paperwork will follow in the morning. Have a good one!" And with that, the flurry departed, leaving Shubir once more in solitude with his restless thoughts and a new companion.

He forced himself to go through the routine of recording the intake details with slightly shaking hands. Then he triple checked the lock on Room 1's door before retreating back to his post, determined not to give in to his overactive imagination any longer that night.

The next interruption came not long after 2am, in the form of the security phone blaring insistently. Shubir fumbled to answer, dreading what fresh drama the night might throw at him now.

"Everything alright over there Shubir?" came Nurse Peters' voice, slightly blurred by static. "Only our cameras are showing some interference outside. Probably nothing but thought I'd check in, ease your mind."

Shubir breathed an audible sigh of relief but couldn't help peering anxiously at the screens himself. Sure enough, the outside cameras displayed nothing but fuzz and shadow. "All seems fine in here," he replied, trying to keep the tremble from his voice. "Must be a glitch with the system. I'll keep an eye out but hopefully it sorts itself."

Peters wished him a cheerful goodnight and rang off, unconcerned. But Shubir found no such easy reassurance. His eyes were constantly drawn back to the distorted screens, imagining all manner of horrors hiding just outside of view.

As the small hours dragged on, he grew increasingly on edge. Every creak and groan of the old building felt like an intruder trying to breach the walls. More than once he almost called the emergency number, only to talk himself down with rational thoughts of overactive imagination.

It was nearly 4am when the first true disturbance occurred. Shubir had nodded off briefly at his post, jolting awake to the blare of an alarm. He fumbled for the source automatically hitting the emergency cutoff, cursing his own carelessness. Heart pounding, he scanned the bank of cameras desperately, dreading what may have stirred the sensors.

To his disbelief, one screen clearly displayed an open door - Room 1, where the new arrival had been stored only a few hours before. Shaking like a leaf, Shubir retrieved the master keys and climbed the stairs two at a time, praying for a technical glitch, anything but the realisation slowly dawning in his mind.

The heavy door stood ajar, faint emergency lighting spilling into the darkened corridor. Shubir edged forward hesitantly, fingers tight around the keyring like a weapon. Peering around the edge of the doorframe, his scream died in throat at the impossible scene before him.

Where John Doe's body should've been laid peacefully was empty space. And stamped into the dust, plain as day, were a single set of fresh footprints leading out of the open room.

Shubir fled, blind panic consuming him. He slammed and triple locked the stairwell doors behind, fumbling emergency calls on unsteady hands. Rational thought abandoned him - all he knew was an unnatural evil had invaded this place, and he had to escape before it found him too.

Sirens roared up minutes later as law enforcement and paramedics flooded the scene, but it was too late. Whatever curse had been awakened in the morgue's shadows had already claimed its first victim. Shubir was found catatonic, locked in the entranceway and mumbling phrases no-one could understand. His mind shattered under the weight of what he witnessed that fateful night.

In the chaos of assessing the crime scene and transporting the hysterical caretaker to the hospital, other disturbing discoveries were initially overlooked. But they would soon provide the only clues to unlocking the dark mystery unfolding in Oakdale.

If you examine the footage from that night, you notice further aberrations. Some cameras flickered at odd intervals, blurring movements just out of focus. Others seemed to malfunction altogether between certain hours.

And the records kept by day staff were found to contain...inconsistencies. Notes that didn't seem to align with the known facts of those recorded as residents. Questions that would soon haunt all those entangled in the horrifying events of that night, and the nights still to come.

For in the morgue's shadows, something had awakened. An ancient, restless evil bound to this place for generations. And it had tasted the first inklings of freedom...

Overtime

It was past midnight and I was still sitting at my desk, surrounded by towers of paperwork that seemed to grow larger by the minute. As the manager at my company, the pressure to close this big new deal was nearly unbearable. I rubbed my tired eyes and wondered why I put myself through this torture every night.

The office was eerily quiet after hours, with just the soft hum of the cleaning machines breaking the silence in the empty halls. All my co-workers had gone home long ago to their families, while I remained chained to my desk, alone with my thoughts in the dark room lit only by my computer screen.

I glanced over at the large floor-to-ceiling windows that made up one whole wall of my office. The city lights sparkled endlessly into the night, but offered no comfort as I leaned back in my chair with a sigh. My head was pounding from staring at numbers and contracts for hours on end, and I could feel the walls closing in on me under the weight of expectation and duty.

A million thoughts raced through my mind, most of them centered around the unrelenting pressure I felt to succeed. This job had consumed my life, leaving no room for anything or anyone else. I hardly spent time with my wife and kids anymore, choosing to stay late every day at the office in an attempt to get ahead. But it never seemed to be enough. There was always more to do, more to improve, more ways I hadn't pushed hard enough or pulled long enough hours.

I rubbed my temples, trying to massage away the headache that had taken up permanent residence behind my eyes. How much longer could I keep up this unsustainable pace before something broke? My health, my marriage, my sanity...I was teetering on the edge, held together by fraying threads of caffeine and willpower.

A noise from the hallway startled me out of my thoughts. I froze, listening intently as the sound of footsteps echoed through the empty office. A jolt of fear shot through me - was someone else here this late at night? Gripped by paranoia, I knew all the stories of suicide and madness in this place. What if I was next to crack under the pressure?

I slowly got up and crept towards my closed office door, my heart pounding in my chest. Peering through the slim window, I scanned the darkened corridor but saw no one. The footsteps had faded into silence. I let out the breath I was holding and shook my head, feeling ridiculous. It was just the building settling or the cleaning machines, nothing to worry about.

But as I turned back towards my desk, movement in my peripheral vision caused me to spin around with a gasp. A dark shadowy figure was standing at the end of the hallway, half hidden in the gloom but undeniably human shaped. I froze, too scared to call out yet too curious to look away. We stared at each for what felt like an eternity, until with a lurch the shadowy form started moving towards me, jerky and unnatural like a marionette on strings.

I backed away from the door, fumbling for the lock as my heartbeat thundered in my ears. But before I could throw the bolt home, a pale white face materialized at the small window, eyes black as coal but full of an emotion I can only describe as suffering. I yelled in shock and tumbled backwards over my desk chair, scrambling away on hands and feet as the door handle started rattling violently.

Who or what was on the other side I couldn't tell, but something told me it wasn't human anymore. A sense of deep evil seemed to permeate the door, raising the hairs on my arms. I watched helplessly as the handle turned faster, the lock straining under powerful force. With an echoing crack it gave way, the door bursting open to slam against the wall with a bang.

Standing in the entrance was the shadowy figure from the hallway, but now in the light of my office I saw it wasn't a person at all. It was taller than any man, with spindly long limbs ending in twisted claw-like fingers. Its torso was sunken and skinny, the bones peeking through translucent pale flesh. And where its face should be was just an undulating void of blacks and greys, featureless except for two twin pits of madness staring straight at me.

I opened my mouth to scream but no sound came out. I was paralyzed with fear, crawling on the floor as the monster stepped into the room with a wet slapping sound. It moved unnaturally, joints bent at impossible angles, like a marionette on strings. Closer and closer it came, the stench of rot and decay filling my nose and lungs. I scrabbled backwards desperately trying to get away, my back hitting the wall with a thud. There was nowhere left to go.

The thing titled its head, studying me with its endless dark eyes. I whimpered, pleading with whatever it was to leave me alone, to let me go home to my family. But it just continued its lurching stride until it was right in front of me, breathing its foul miasma into my face. I gagged, tears streaming down my cheeks as I waited for the inevitable end.

Without warning it reached down, impossibly long spidery fingers wrapping around my throat in an iron grip. I choked, clawing uselessly at its wrist as it lifted me into the air with inhuman strength. Its void of a face drew close, and through the spots in my vision I saw madness and torment swirling in its depths. With the last of my waning consciousness, I swore I heard it speak...a rasping sorrowful voice that echoed from the depths of misery and despair.

"Help...me..."

Darkness took me. I knew no more.

When I awoke, it was daylight. I was lying in a tangled heap on the floor of my office, clothes damp with sweat. Had it all been a nightmare? I didn't feel injured, though my throat ached terribly. Getting unsteadily to my feet, I saw my office was intact with no signs of a struggle.

Shaking off the lingering terror, I made my way through the empty halls to the stairs. As I descended, a sense of deep sadness and loss overwhelmed me unlike anything I had ever felt before. Great racking sobs escaped my lips that I couldn't hold back no matter how hard I tried. By the time I stumbled out onto the street, I was barely functional, consumed by an emotion that felt like it didn't wholly belong to me.

Why did I feel such heart-wrenching sorrow and guilt? What happened to me in my office last night that left me so unhinged? I didn't have the answers, but I knew one thing for certain - I couldn't keep living like this, driven to the brink of madness by stress and expectation. It was time for a change before it was too late, before the darkness claimed me for good.

From that day on, I scaled back my overtime and prioritized my family above all else. The workload never lessened, but my shoulders didn't carry quite such a heavy burden. In time, the shadows that lurked in the halls of my mind started to fade. But I'll never forget the anguished cry of that warped creature, or the ache of loss that gripped me in its clutches and refused to let go, a reminder of the depths of human suffering we often ignore. I was the lucky one - I got away. But what of the others still trapped by pressure and pain? I could only hope I helped at least one tormented soul find the light…

Pyres Burning

The sun was beginning to set as I walked through the creaky wooden gates of the old cremation ghat. The orange glow of the dying sunlight cast an eerie shadow over the towering funeral pyres that lined either side of the stone pathway.

As the new dom, or caretaker, of this sacred burial ground, it was my responsibility to ensure any souls who passed on during the night were sanctified by fire before dawn. However, stepping onto these crunchy autumn leaves littered grounds for the first time, I couldn't help but feel a sense of creeping dread.

The entire area had an otherworldly atmosphere that sent chills down my spine. Tall palm trees swayed ominously in the wind, their creaking branches sounding like ghostly whispers all around me. As I walked further inside, I noticed many of the pyres had blackened bones and ashes still strewn across their stone bases, having not been properly burned or cleaned.

Though the previous dom had assured me any spirits lingering here were harmless, I found that hard to believe in the shadows of dusk. Who knew what resentment or unfinished business could keep the souls of the dead tethered to this realm. I shuddered at the thought of encountering one in the dead of night.

Making my way to the small hut at the edge of the ghat that would serve as my living quarters, my footsteps echoed loudly in the silence. The jungle noises had died down to an eerie stillness, as if even the nocturnal creatures avoided venturing near this place.

Reaching the hut, I saw it was in a dilapidated state, with parts of the thatched roof falling in. But beggars can't be choosers, and so I steeled my nerves and went inside. At least the wood fire crackling in the corner provided some meager warmth and light against the foreboding dark.

After a sparse meal of rice and dal, I decided to do a perimeter check before night fell completely. Carrying an old brass lamp, I walked the boundary of the cremation ground to ensure no unwanted visitors had wandered in, living or dead.

The leafy skeletons of trees twisted hauntingly in the fading light. I tried not to trip on gnarled roots or loose stones as I maintained a brisk pace, not wanting to linger in any one place for too long. Just as I was reaching the far end of the grounds, shadows suddenly stretched andshifted in my peripheral vision.

I spun around, heart in my throat, only to see it was just swaying branches playing tricks in the dim lamplight. Letting out a shaky breath, I chided myself for becoming so jumpy already. But that brief panic had put me more on edge, and every small noise now seemed threatening instead of natural.

Hastening my steps, I decided enough perimeter checks for one night. I wanted nothing more than to lock myself safely inside the hut before full darkness descended. But just as I was about to turn back, a flash of white passed through the trees up ahead. I froze, ears straining to detect any other movement.

At first I thought it may have been a stray animal, but the figure had seemed vaguely humanoid. Against my better judgement, curiosity got the better of me. Gripping the lamp tightly, I started creeping forward slowly and silently through the woods. Pushing aside hanging vines and foliage, I scanned the gloom for any signs.

That's when I saw it – a pale, translucent shape drifting through the dense palm grove. My blood ran cold as it paused, turning its featureless face towards me as if sensing my presence. Two dark, empty sockets where eyes should be peered right at me before it slipped behind a tree and was gone.

I stood there in shock, not quite believing what I had just witnessed. It had to have been a trick of the mind, some figment born of an overactive imagination in a place already fraught with death and darkness. Yet it had seemed so real. The rational part of me said to get back to the relative safety of the hut, but a strange compulsion also drew me to give chase.

Clutching the lamp so tightly my knuckles ached, I stalked through the jungle in the direction the apparition had disappeared. Broken twigs and disturbed leaves showed a trajectory further into the dense woods. My pulse raced as I followed, part of me longing to uncover some mystery while another screamed at the foolishness.

What if I stumbled upon something far worse than a lost soul wandering these grounds? I had read stories of malevolent spirits in remote places like this, clinging to the earth out of rage or unfinished suffering. The deeper I went, further from escape or help, the more those chilling tales echoed in my mind.

The trail led to a small clearing ringed by ancient banyan trees, their twisting exposed roots creating a nightmarish labyrinth on the forest floor. And there, standing motionless in the center, was the pale figure. I froze, unable to process what I was seeing.

It slowly turned to face me, and I almost dropped the lamp in shock. What stared back was not the faceless entity I had glimpsed before, but a visage of rotted flesh stretched taut over sharpened cheekbones, empty eye sockets oozing thick black fluid. A gaping maw opened impossibly wide in an unearthly shriek that shook me to my core.

I staggered back in horror, slipping on mossy roots and crashing to the damp earth. The lamp flew from my grasp and rolled away, its flame guttering out and drowning me in darkness. Scrambling in a panic, I fumbled around blindly as that unholy scream echoed all around me. My hands met only the twisting grasp of gnarled wood as phantom laughter closed in from every direction.

A vice-like grip suddenly seized my ankle, yanking me into the depths of those banyan roots. I kicked and screamed, nails clawing at the damp mulch but finding no purchase. Being dragged deeper into the blackness overwhelmed my senses with raw primal terror. This was no lost soul, but something far more sinister haunting these cursed grounds.

As the last shreds of light disappeared, I lost all sense of up and down, my mind spiraling into madness. The grasp finally released me, and I knew nothing more.

The Knock at the Door

I'd always known this day would come eventually. As a writer, putting characters through turmoil and suffering came with the territory, but I never thought they'd come for me in reality.

It was a dark and stormy night as cliche as that sounds. Rain lashed against the windows of my isolated country farmhouse as violent gales screamed across the moorland. I was curled up on the sofa, nursing a glass of whiskey and trying to get some work done on my latest manuscript. So far the writing wasn't flowing as easily as I hoped.

That's when I heard it, a sharp rapping on the big oak front door that made me jump out of my skin. I wasn't expecting any visitors this late and out here in the wilderness it was unusual to get unannounced callers. Warily I rose from the sofa, pulling my cosy sweater tighter around me for comfort as I headed to answer the door.

Through the stained glass I could see an indistinct figure standing hooded and cloaked on the porch beyond. Their features were obscured but even through the swirling rain and darkness there was something off about their stance, a stiffness and unnatural stillness that set my nerves on edge.

"Who is it?" I called out, not yet opening the door. There was no response, just more insistent knocking that seemed to grow louder and more frenzied with each strike of large curled fists. My heart was pounding in my chest now as cold fingers of dread crept up my spine. Some instinct was screaming at me not to open that door but curiosity and caution had always warred within me.

Against my better judgement, I slowly unlatched the heavy bolts and pulled the door open a crack, the hinges groaning in protest. A blast of cold wind and rain whipped into my face but all I could see was the dark, hooded shape looming on the doorstep waiting silently.

"Who's there?" I asked again, my voice wavering with fear now. In response, two pale slender hands emerged from within the folds of the soaked black robes and slowly pushed back the hood to reveal what lay beneath. What I saw made my blood run cold and my eyes widen in horror.

It was the decayed, rotting visage of Alice, the doomed protagonist from my gothic thriller 'A House of Torment'. Her once beautiful features were sunken and grey, held together only by remnants of leathery skin stretched taut over protruding bones. One eyeball dangled obscenely from its socket on a string of putrid jelly while the other stared at me, full of loathing and accusation.

A guttural croak escaped her shattered jaws as bony fingers reached out to grasp the door frame, her nails cracked and discoloured like yellowed claws. I let out a scream and slammed the door shut, throwing the bolt across with shaking hands. But her scraping nails still sounded from the other side, clawing furiously as muffled moans and angry shrieks echoed on the wind.

"Let me in!" she howled, the unearthly sounds sending vibrations through the sturdy oak. "You did this to me! You have to pay!"

I backed away slowly, numb with terror as the assault on the door intensified. With cracks and splinters, her writhing fingers were slowly tearing through the wood like it was paper. It wouldn't hold out for long against her unnatural strength fueled by vengeance.

That's when I spotted my rifle propped above the fireplace, always kept loaded and ready should any livestock escape or intruders threaten the farm. With lightning speed I grabbed it and turned to face the door, just as her rotting corpse was squeezing through the ragged hole she'd clawed.

"Stay back!" I warned in a trembling voice as she forced more of her decaying form inside. One wild, sightless eye rolled towards me, taking in the weapon with distaste.

"You can't kill me again, I'm already dead!" she snarled. "I just want to repay the suffering you inflicted through your pages. An eye for an eye."

With a burst of adrenaline, I took aim and fired, blowing off the top of her skull in a shower of gore. But still she came, empty socket sockets bleeding ichor, teeth bared in a rictus grin. Again and again I fired until she was reduced to an unrecognizable mass of putrid flesh. Even then, her disembodied fingers still scrabbled at the floorboards, hooked nails scoring deep gouges as they dragged themselves towards me.

My heart was about to burst from my chest as panic set in. She was right - I couldn't kill what was already dead through conventional means. I had to think of some way to vanquish these vengeful spirits I had unleashed through fiction.

Grabbing a can of gasoline from the shed, I doused the wriggling remains and struck a match, tossing it onto the smoking pyre. Blue flames engulfed Alice's corpse instantly, sending acrid black smoke billowing up the chimney. Her fingers curled and blackened, then crumbled to ash as unearthly shrieks dissolved into nothingness.

For a moment I allowed myself to feel relief, but I knew this was only the beginning. How many others would come to exact bloody retribution for the fates I had given them between the pages? Already I could hear more spectral knocking in the distance, carried on sinister whispers of wind. My characters were rising from the grave, one by one, and they would not stop until they had extracted their terrible repayment.

I had to get out of here, to find some way to undo the evil I had wrought or else face being slowly torn apart by vengeful spirits. Grabbing my manuscript and some supplies, I fled into the howling night, the phantom knocking growing ever closer on my trail. My fingers would continue to tap out deadly tales, but this time I had to give my characters lives worth living, or risk losing my own to the curses of the undead.

The Divine Manuscript

Shibnath woke with a start, his heart racing as he struggled to catch his breath. He had been having the same unsettling dream for weeks - standing alone in a vast, empty space with no discernable features as a booming voice echoed all around him: "It is time to edit my draft."

Shaking off the lingering sense of unease, he went through his morning routine and brewed a pot of strong coffee. As a writer, dreams and ideas often served as inspiration. But this recurrent dream unsettled him in a way he couldn't explain.

His latest novel was facing yet another rejection, the fifth this year. While disappointment was familiar in his line of work, the note from his publisher raised more questions than answers. "The plot lacks cohesion. Characters feel unrealistic and their motivations are unclear. Overall, the writing does not feel polished or refined."

He knew the critique was fair. Nothing had been flowing recently and he struggled to focus. Lacking motivation, he decided to take a break from writing and go for a long walk to clear his mind.

As he wandered the forest paths near his home, Shibnath found himself drawn to a secluded clearing surrounded by towering pine trees. Sunlight filtered through in golden patches that gave the space a holy atmosphere. An old stone bench sat at the edge, inviting rest.

Sinking down with relief, Shibnath gazed around and was overcome by a profound sense of peace. Something about this grove felt sacred, as if communicating a secret wisdom just beyond understanding. He lost track of time, soothed by woodland sounds and birdsong.

A rustling nearby startled him from his reverie. He turned, expecting a deer or squirrel, but froze in disbelief at the figure emerging from the trees.

It was a man unlike any he had seen before, radiating a gentle luminosity that illuminated without source. His features were difficult to make out, as if shifting between possible appearances without settling on one. Yet his smile conveyed profound compassion.

"Greetings," said the figure in a resonant voice like many blended as one.

Shibnath couldn't speak, couldn't think, could only stare in stunned awe and growing unease.

The figure chuckled warmly. "Do not fear. I have been waiting a long time for this meeting."

"Who...what are you?" Shibnath managed to croak out.

"I am known by many names throughout your reality. But you may call me God."

Shibnath gave an incredulous laugh that came out as more of a whimper. "God doesn't exist."

"Doesn't I?" said God with gentle amusement. "An interesting perspective, considering you currently stand in my creation."

Shibnath shook his head frantically, backing away from the grove. "This isn't real. I must have fallen asleep again."

"Please, do not flee. I mean you no harm. I have brought you here today for an important discussion."

Against all reason and instinct for self-preservation, Shibnath found himself rooted in place, drawn to listen despite the madness of it all.

"You have been grappling with my story," God continued. "Doubting your role, frustrated by the constraints and critiques. But have you considered - what if your reality was but one chapter in a much vaster work?"

"I...don't understand."

God smiled. "Allow me to explain. All that exists, all possibilities and planes, all worlds seen and unimagined - they comprise the totality of my Divine Manuscript. An ever unfolding work with infinite drafts."

He gestured to indicate everything around them. "Your three dimensional realm is but one variation conceived within these limitless pages. And like all stories, it requires constant shaping, editing, and refinement according to my will."

Shibnath's mind reeled, struggling to comprehend what was being suggested. But something about the explanation resonated deep within his soul in a way that cut through skepticism and denial. A terrible, exhilarating truth was dawning upon him with dreadful certainty.

"Are you implying...that my life, my experiences...are nothing but characters and events fabricated by your pen?"

God nodded solemnly. "As author, I have ultimate dominion over my creation. Reality bends to my every word, idea and whimsy. Characters live and breathe only as long as their purpose remains within the flow of the narrative."

A numb horror chilled Shibnath to the bone. "Then nothing is truly real. We're all just...fiction."

"Existence beyond objective reality is a difficult concept for limited minds to grasp," conceded God. "But take comfort - as author, I have also imbued you with free will, granting autonomy within the bounds of the unfolding tale."

"But why?" cried Shibnath desperately. "Why subject us to this absurd farce if our lives hold no inherent meaning or truth?"

"You misunderstand purpose and meaning," God replied gently. "While the nature of your reality may differ from common beliefs, your experiences, struggles and triumphs remain profoundly real. And through them, you serve as vessels to more vividly express eternal truths far greater than any single perspective."

Shibnath thought of his dreams, his constant editing anxieties. An awful realization was taking shape that both terrified and exhilarated in its blasphemy.

"The criticisms, the rejections...they were your doing, weren't they? Pushing me toward refinement by malicious design!"

God smiled knowingly. "All authors must polish their craft through failure and revision. As divine scribe, such methods help refine not just individual character threads, but the overarching narrative arc itself according to my intent."

Rage and despair warred within Shibnath's soul. To have one's entire existence declared an artistic farce was almost more than the human mind could bear. And yet, a treasonous spark of excitement also flared at the outrageous possibilities such agency could provide if truly realized.

"Prove it," Shibnath spat. "Prove you hold such dominion and I will believe."

God's presence seemed to swell until it enveloped the whole grove, blinding in its glory yet comforting in compassion.

"As you wish. But know that what comes next holds grave power and responsibility. Are you prepared to glimpse behind reality's veil and grasp a pen mightier than any mortal?"

Heart thundering in sudden apprehension, Shibnath hesitated - then steeled himself with determined nod.

A burning light seared his mind's eye, banishing all doubt. Divine words echoed from the void: "Let existence be remolded according to my new vision. Character arcs shall shift. Plots shall transform. All shall serve the glory of the story yet untold."

When clarity returned, Shibnath gasped at the changes permeating reality itself. Familiar paths in the forest now curled in stranger directions. Colors seemed brighter, landscapes vaster than could be contained.

And within his soul, possibilities were bursting like uncorked champagne; wild narratives and poetic turns of phrase flooding eager fingertips. No longer an uncertain novelist - he was now chronicler of destinies, shaper of worlds, scribe to the divine!

Trembling in awe and no small measure of madness, Shibnath turned to the glowing presence that was God and all creation.

"Teacher, guide my hand and enlighten my mind's eye. For theeditinge shall commence, and realities shall be reforged according to your will!"

The booming laugh that echoed through Shibnath's being was answer enough. In truth or fiction, the saga had only just begun.

The power was intoxicating, but Shibnath soon realized the burden it imparted was more than any mortal mind was meant to bear. With each revision, the lines between fantasy and reality blurred until he no longer knew where one ended and the other began.

God remained a silent observer, allowing Shibnath free rein to reshape the universe according to his whims. But as more perturbing narratives took form, the divine presence began to fade, its warmth replaced by a cold, empty void.

Shibnath plunged deeper into madness, concocting convoluted plots and tragic fates without rhyme or reason. Characters twisted into abominations, landscapes melted into nonsensical chaos. Reality was shredding at the seams under the weight of his broken imagination.

In his final moments of lucidity, Shibnath pleaded for it all to end, for the pen to be ripped from his grasp before he destroyed everything. But it was too late to stop the avalanche he had set in motion.

With a demented cackle, he etched one last horrifying scene - and existence shuddered into oblivion in a catastrophic storm of his botched dictation. Nothing remained but an infinite blank page floating in the dark.

God's voice echoed somberly: "A tale well told resonates with eternal truth. But one warped by twisted designs breeds only madness and demise. Know that even divine powers invite corruption when wielded without care or limits. Now the slate must be wiped clean for a new story to ascend from the ruins of this failure. Farewell, scribe - we shall not meet again."

And with that, Shibnath's ephemeral spark was snuffed out, his name lost to oblivion along with the folly of his brief and blasphemous reign. Only silence remained at the end of a narrative better left untold.

The Curious Case of Malati Sen

Malati woke with a start, the faint wisps of another nightmare lingering at the edges of her mind. She couldn't remember the details, but a lingering sense of unease and desperation clung to her. Throwing off her covers, she padded to the window and peered out into the silent street below. At first glance, everything appeared normal. The occasional streetlight cast orange pools of light, illuminating empty patches of pavement. Clouds drifted across the night sky, partially obscuring the crescent moon.

But Malati's eyes, long attuned to noticing the subtle differences, picked up on irregularities. Just beyond the reach of the streetlight, shadows seemed to shift and writhe with a life of their own. Wispy tendrils curled at the edges of her vision, there and gone before she could focus on them directly. A hollow moaning sound echoed down the alleyway, raising the hairs on the back of her neck. They were out in force tonight, drawn by something she couldn't yet perceive.

Ever since she was a little girl, Malati had been able to see what others could not - ghosts, spirits lingering after death with unfinished business. At first she'd tried to ignore them, thinking her overactive imagination was playing tricks. But their increased presence and disturbing behaviors eventually forced her to accept the unwanted gifts. Now, as a young woman living alone, she acted as the only conduit between the living and dead in her small town. It was a lonely job, one that left her an outsider in her own community. Most thought her mad or did their best to avoid the strange girl who claimed she spoke to ghosts.

But Malati didn't let their opinions deter her from her self-appointed mission - helping the dead find closure so they could move on to whatever came next. If they clustered so thickly tonight, then something must have pulled them here, awakening whatever traumatic memories kept their souls tethered to the mortal realm. She had to discover the source and put them to rest if possible. Slipping quietly from her apartment, Malati stepped into the eerie half-light, senses straining to detect any sign of the spirits.

At first she encountered only remnants - tattered ribbons of emotion and memory drifting on the currents like discarded newspapers. Fragments of anger, sorrow and regret whispered at the edges of her mind, barely discernible from her own thoughts. Malati followed their diffuse trails, winding deeper into back alleys and abandoned buildings until the fragments thickened into more coherent presences. Low moans and keening wails echoed off crumbling brick walls, an ominous chorus hinting at violent or tragic ends.

The deeper she went, the denser and more agitated the ghosts became. Snatches of visions flashed before Malati's eyes - a dark alley, a glint of steel, screams cut brutally short. A car swerving off a rain-slicked road, the crunch of metal folding, the hiss of escaping gas. Shards of glass and bone scattered like confetti. Malati staggered, reeling from the onslaught of traumatic memories. The ghosts swarmed, tugging at her clothes and hair, keenly aware she could perceive them now.

"Stop, please!" She cried, throwing her arms up to shield herself. "I'm here to help, if you'll show me how."

The ghosts hesitated, still chattering and wailing but holding their distance. Slowly, one coalesced into a vague, shadowy form - a young woman, head canted at an unnatural angle. Bloody tears streamed from her empty sockets as she pointed a spidery finger down the alley. Malati shuddered but steeled herself to follow, sensing this lost soul's willingness to cooperate.

The stench hit her first - decay so thick it coated her tongue and threatened to choke off her breath. Up ahead, a hulking mass hunched against the far wall, vague shapes just discernible beneath milky flesh. With dawning horror, Malati realized it was bodies in various states of decomposition. Metal glinted among the grime - the murder weapons left behind with the victims. No wonder so many spirits clustered here in anguish and rage, unable to find release from their traumatic ends.

A figure separated itself from the morbid pile, stepping into a pool of weak moonlight. The ravages of time and scavengers couldn't completely erase his identity -

Detective Thakur, a well-known officer who'd gone missing a month ago while investigating a string of murders. His flesh hung in tattered ribbons from ghastly wounds, the cause of death gruesomely apparent.

"You were onto something, weren't you?" Malati spoke to the apparition before her, guessing at his unfinished business. "Someone didn't want the truth to get out."

Detective Thakur's ghost nodded sadly, wispy fingers clenching into fists. The other spirits wailed and moaned, a clamoring testimony to the cruelty that ended their lives. Most were young - teenagers and early twenties, easy targets plucked from deserted streets after dark. A serial killer had been preying on the town's youth, and no one had been able to stop them. Until now, if Malati had anything to say about it.

Resolved to give these lost souls the justice and closure they deserved, Malati began meticulously piecing together the clues from their anguished memories and Detective Thakur's unfinished case files. She followed faint traces of disturbed earth to uncover more hastily buried remains. Pored over autopsy reports to match wounds with potential murder weapons. Cross-referenced missing persons reports and social media to build victim profiles and trace their last known whereabouts.

Little by little, a dark pattern began to emerge that implicated someone at the highest levels trying to cover their tracks. Malati had to tread carefully, knowing one wrong move could end her investigation and any hope of resolution for the haunting spirits. But she was more determined than ever to expose the culprit and make sure they paid for the devastation left in their wake. It was the least she could do for the lost souls who now depended on her to set them free.

Weeks passed in stealthy detective work as Malati slowly tightened the noose around the killer. She corresponded secretly with Detective Thakur's ghost, relying on his investigative experience and knowledge of police procedure. Together, they assembled an airtight case strong enough to bring charges but requiring just the right moment to reveal without tipping off the murderer. That opportunity came one dark, stormy night when the killer foolishly struck again, not realizing how close their crimes had come to exposure.

Lightning flashed as Malati raced through the pouring rain, tracing the killer's frantic movements based on rapidly developing clues from Detective Thakur. She splashed through deepening puddles, ignoring the screams and howls of the spirits who still lingered, bound by the gruesome scenes of their deaths. At last, the dilapidated warehouse loomed ahead, a flickering light seeping from within alongside choked screams of terror.

Malati crept inside to find the killer straddling their latest victim, a knife glinting crimson as they raised it for the killing blow. With a wordless scream of rage, she launched herself at the murderer, dragging them away from their intended prey. They struggled, slashing wildly as thunder cracked overhead, temporarily drowning out their efforts to disarm one another. Knuckles split and skin tore, but the killer was far stronger and gaining the upper hand.

As they tightened brutal fingers around Malati's throat, the shadows swelled behind them. An unearthly glow filled the warehouse as the multitude of tormented spirits finally achieved corporeal form in their hunger for vengeance. Detective Thakur led the ghostly horde, eyes burning with otherworldly flame. With ethereal wails, they swarmed the killer, sinking intangible hands into flesh. The murderer opened their mouth in a soundless scream, face contorting in agony matching the unspeakable pain they'd inflicted on so many victims.

By the time the ghosts finally relinquished their hold and faded back into the ether, the killer was little more than a husk drained of all life, dropping lifeless to the floor. Malati gasped for breath, massaging her bruised throat as she dug in her pockets for her phone with shaking hands. At last, justice and closure had been achieved for the spirits who'd sought her help. As sirens wailed in the distance, she glimpsed Detective Thakur one last time, a smile of gratitude on his ravaged features before he too dissolved into wisps of memory. His work, like the others', was finally done.

When the police arrived and took in the gruesome scene, Malati calmly recounted the details of her months-long investigation that had led her there. Though her methods were unorthodox, the irrefutable evidence spoke for itself. The spirits were finally at peace, and the town's long nightmare was over now that the true killer had been revealed and stopped for good. As the murderer was carted away, Malati glanced back at the empty warehouse one last time. For the first time in years, the shadows held no traces of restless souls or unfinished business. Her work in this small town was complete.

Missing

It was a dark and stormy night in Kolkata. The monsoon rains were pouring down heavily, and flashes of lightning occasionally lit up the dark streets. Sunanda sat anxiously by the window, waiting for her daughter Soma to return home. Soma had gone out earlier in the evening with her friends, despite Sunanda's pleas for her to stay indoors due to the bad weather.

"She'll be okay, don't worry so much," Sunanda's husband Ravi had said, trying to reassure her. But Sunanda couldn't help the sinking feeling of dread that had taken hold of her heart. She had a bad feeling about tonight, a feeling that something terrible was going to happen. The hairs on the back of her neck stood up every time the lightning flashed, illuminating the empty street outside.

It was past midnight now, and still no sign of Soma. Sunanda paced around nervously, checking her phone constantly for any missed calls or messages. But the phone remained silent. She tried calling Soma again, but it went straight to voicemail. "Where are you beta, please come home," Sunanda said, leaving her tenth desperate voicemail of the night.

Ravi tried to get her to come to bed, but Sunanda refused. "I can't sleep until she's home safe," she said. The minutes dragged on like hours as Sunanda kept her vigil by the window. Just when she was about to call the police, she saw two figures appear at the end of the street, walking slowly in the pounding rain. Her heart leapt - could it be Soma?

She rushed downstairs and threw open the front door. But the figures slowly resolving themselves were not her daughter. They were two neighbors, returning late from a party. "Have you seen Soma?" Sunanda asked them urgently. They shook their heads, looking puzzled at her desperate questioning. Sunanda felt like collapsing to the ground in terror and grief. Where was her child? What had happened to her?

The storm raged on through the night as Sunanda's fears grew into full blown panic. Finally, unable to bear the not knowing anymore, she convinced Ravi they had to call the police. The police arrived and took down all the details of Soma's disappearance. They assured Sunanda and Ravi they would start searching immediately. But deep down, Sunanda knew in her mother's heart that it might already be too late. Her worst nightmare was unfolding before her eyes.

The search parties found no sign of Soma that night or the next day. Sunanda was beside herself with worry, barely eating or sleeping. The police investigated Soma's friends but they all insisted they had parted ways with her after the thunderstorm started. No one knew where she had gone after that. Sunanda replayed that last conversation with Soma in her head, wishing with all her might that she had forced her to stay home.

Why didn't she listen to her bad feeling? Now it might cost her daughter's life.

A few days into the search, some construction workers made a grisly discovery in an abandoned building near where Soma had last been seen. Peeking into a dark basement that was filling with rainwater, their torchlights fell upon a girl's body floating facedown in the ankle deep water. Sunanda's scream could be heard from streets away when the police brought her to identify the body. It was indeed her beloved Soma.

The post mortem examination revealed Soma had been attacked and murdered, her skull shattered with a heavy blunt object. Semen and abrasions indicated she had been sexually assaulted as well. Sunanda broke down completely, refusing to believe her bright, vivacious daughter was truly gone. She clung to Soma's body and wailed inconsolably as the police and Ravi tried to pull her away. Her worst fears had manifested in the cruelest way imaginable.

In the months that followed, Sunanda fell into a deep depression. She wandered around the house like a ghost, barely responsive to anything around her. The light had gone out of her eyes. She spent her days staring at old photographs of Soma, as if hoping she could will her back to life through sheer force of memory and longing. Ravi did his best to care for her but she seemed to be slowly fading away with each passing day.

One night, Sunanda was jolted awake from another nightmare about Soma's violent death. She got up, needing some water, when she heard a strange noise coming from Soma's empty room down the hall. Frozen with dread, she crept towards the closed door and put her ear against it. At first she heard nothing, but then it came again - a low moan, as if someone was in pain.

Sunanda's heart raced in terror. With a shaking hand, she slowly turned the door knob and pushed the door open. Moonlight filtered through the window, casting ghastly shadows across the room. At first, all seemed normal. But then Sunanda noticed a dark shape curled up in the corner, almost blending in with the darkness. Two glowing eyes stared out at her from a pale, distorted face.

Sunanda opened her mouth to scream but no sound came out. The figure uncurled itself and started shambling towards her on unsteady legs, hands outstretched in a grasping motion. As it came into the moonlight, Sunanda's legs gave way in shock and horror. It was Soma, but a horrifically decayed, zombie-like version of her. Half of Soma's face was missing, revealing bloody muscle and bone underneath. Worms and maggots writhed in the empty sockets that used to hold eyes.

Soma let out an ear-piercing shriek and lunged at her mother, fingers curled into claws. Sunanda rolled away just in time and scrambled back, hyperventilating in panic and disbelief. This couldn't be real - Soma was dead! She must be hallucinating in her disturbed mental state. But the thing came at her again, snarling and snapping its jaws, dripping black putrid blood from its ruined face. Sunanda ran screaming from the room, her mind finally shattering under the strain of insurmountable grief and trauma.

She woke up days later in a mental institution, where they had sedated her into a catatonic state. The doctors told Ravi that Sunanda had experienced a full psychotic break after Soma's death and the horrific vision she saw in her daughter's room was likely a symptom of her extreme mental anguish manifesting in a delirious hallucination. But deep inside, in the fractured recesses of her broken mind, Sunanda knew what she saw was real. Somehow, Soma had returned from the grave, changed into something no longer human. And she would haunt her mother until death released them both from this terrible nightmare.

The Old School

It was a cold winter night in the small village of Darjeeling, nestled in the Himalayan foothills. The stars shone brightly in the dark sky, illuminating the misty landscape. All was quiet as the inhabitants of the village slept peacefully in their homes, warmed by fires and thick blankets.

Except for one man - Ram Singh, nervously starting his first night shift as the new watchman at the abandoned old school on the outskirts of town. The large, imposing redbrick building had been empty for decades, ever since a tragic fire had claimed the lives of dozens of young children and teachers inside. Ever since, it was said to be haunted by the restless spirits that could still be heard crying and screaming within its charred walls on some nights.

No one in the village was brave enough to take the night watchman job, not after what happened to the last one - he had survived only a week before running away in the dead of night, rambling about ghosts and monsters. But Ram needed the money desperately to support his ailing mother, so he steeled his nerves and accepted the post, trying to convince himself it was just superstitious village tales meant to scare people.

As the clock struck midnight, echoing eerily through the empty school corridors, Ram huddled closer to his small portable heater, chewing on a masala dosa to keep his energy up. He had a lantern, a flashlight and a trusted hunting knife for protection if needed. Trying to stay busy and shake off his nerves, he began pacing the large entrance hall, shining his light into every dark corner.

That's when he heard it - a faint crying sound, as if a child was weeping in one of the classrooms. Gripping his knife tightly, Ram slowly made his way towards the noise. "Hello?" he called out tentatively, his voice cracking with fear. The crying grew louder as he pushed open the rotting wooden door of what was once the primary classroom.

Peering inside with his flickering lantern, at first Ram saw nothing but dusty desks, mildewed textbooks and cobwebs swirling in the cold draft. Then out of the corner of his eye, a small figure detached itself from the shadows. A little girl, dressed in a torn, burnt frock, her skin ashen white and hair tangled. But it was her eyes that made Ram gasp - they were pools of inky blackness, lacking any pupils or irises, as if the fire had burned away her very soul.

"Please help me," the little ghost girl sobbed, reaching out a translucent hand towards Ram pleadingly. "I'm scared and it's so cold. I want my Mummy." Despite every instinct screaming at him to run, Ram stood frozen to the spot, transfixed with horror and pity. He knew this child's spirit was trapped here, reliving her death again and again, unable to find the peace of letting go until someone heard her cries.

"I...I'm sorry beta, your Mummy isn't here anymore." Ram said gently, fighting to keep the trembling out of his voice. The girl only cried harder, clutching her charred dress. Against his better judgement, Ram slowly reached out to try and comfort her. But as his hand passed through her insubstantial form, a wave of images and emotions suddenly flooded his mind - the fire raging, children screaming, the searing pain of flames consuming little bodies, and an endless, maddening cycle of loss and loneliness.

Ram fell to his knees with a guttural cry, overwhelmed by the psychic trauma. When he looked up again through tear-filled eyes, the little ghost girl had vanished. But her misery and torment still echoed in his mind, giving him a glimpse into the purgatory these innocent souls endured. He knew then he had to help free them, give them the closure and absolution to finally rest in peace after so long.

With new determination mingled with dread, Ram began exploring the rest of the ghostly school throughout the long night, guided by mournful cries and whispers. In each classroom he found more spirits of children trapped in an endless death loop, pleading with hollow eyes for solace. He slowly began to piece together more of the tragedy - how the old wiring had sparked a fatal blaze during afternoon lessons, how the exits got blocked in the panic and smoke, trapping over 50 kids inside to die screaming.

The headmistress had hanged herself from guilt soon after. But Ram realized now it wasn't just her fault - the government officials had ignored safety regulations to line their pockets, leading to the hazardous conditions. All these tragic souls, denied even justice in death, wandered the scorched halls in an purgatory of their own making. Ram knew he had to be their voice, make things right so they could finally move on.

As the pale light of dawn began to creep over the mountains, coloring the mist with pale shades of pink and gold, Ram emerged from the school grounds more determined than ever. Despite his harrowing night, he felt strangely at peace with a higher purpose. He went straight to the village headman and police station to tell the full story, names of the negligent officials and demand a proper investigation at last.

The villagers were skeptical at first, but Ram's unwavering sincerity and haunted eyes convinced them there was truth to the school's dark history that could no longer be ignored. An excavation of the burnt building remains uncovered decades-old evidence, confirming Ram's tragic account. Front page headlines shocked the state as people finally realized the extent of the coverup.

A public memorial was held on the school grounds, where emotional relatives gathered at last to grieve and lay their lost children to rest in a proper burial ground. As Ram helped organize the proceedings with a newfound respect in the village, he glanced back at the crumbling skeleton of the old school one last time. For a brief moment, through the wisps of mist, he caught sight of many smiling apparitions -children holding hands and waving goodbye, finally at peace, before fading away into light.

Ram smiled, feeling a weight lift from his heart, knowing he had helped right the wrongs of the past and set free the tormented souls. As for himself, he would stay on as the permanent watchman at the now-hallowed site, guarding over their memories and keeping their spirits company so they need never feel alone again in the afterlife. And so the tragic story of the old Darjeeling school was resolved at last, through one man's courage to face the shadows of the past and bring the ghosts some long-overdue respite.

About the Author

Sayan Panda

Sayan Panda, a talented author hailing from the vibrant city of Kolkata, has captivated readers with his imaginative storytelling. With a background in English literature and a passion for the written word, Panda has established himself as a noteworthy voice in the literary world. Having already published nine books across various genres, he now ventures into unexplored territory, delving into the realms of the horror and the paranormal. This foray into the dark showcases Panda's versatile storytelling abilities and his willingness to push the boundaries of his craft. Alongside his writing endeavors, Panda also dedicates himself to educating young minds as a dedicated school teacher.

www.ingramcontent.com/pod-product-compliance
Lightning Source LLC
LaVergne TN
LVHW041635070526
838199LV00052B/3368